The Wildlife ABC

A Nature Alphabet Book

Jan Thornhill

Owl kids

Owlkids Books Inc.
10 Lower Spadina Avenue, Suite 400, Toronto, Ontario M5V 2Z2
www.owlkids.com

Text and illustrations © 2012 Jan Thornhill

This book contains material that has previously appeared in
The Wildlife ABC: A Nature Alphabet © 1988
and *The Wildlife ABC & 123: A Nature Alphabet & Counting Book* © 2004

Distributed in Canada by University of Toronto Press
5201 Dufferin Street, Toronto, Ontario M3H 5T8

Distributed in the United States by Publishers Group West
1700 Fourth Street, Berkeley, California 94710

Library and Archives Canada Cataloguing in Publication

Thornhill, Jan
     The wildlife ABC : a nature alphabet book / Jan Thornhill.

Issued also in electronic format.
ISBN 978-1-926973-08-1

     1. Animals--Juvenile literature. 2. English language--Alphabet--
Juvenile literature. 3. Alphabet books. I. Title.

QL49.T5625 2012   j590   C2011-904969-4

Design and art direction: Wycliffe Smith, Claudia Dávila
Illustrations: Jan Thornhill

Canada Council   Conseil des Arts   ONTARIO ARTS COUNCIL
for the Arts   du Canada   CONSEIL DES ARTS DE L'ONTARIO

We acknowledge the financial support of the Canada Council for the Arts, the Government of Canada through
the Canada Book Fund, the Ontario Arts Council, and the Ontario Media Development Corporation.

Manufactured by WKT Co. Ltd.
Manufactured in Shenzhen, Guangdong, China in July 2011
Job #11CB1515

A   B   C   D   E   F

 Publisher of Chirp, chickaDEE and OWL
www.owlkids.com

Aa

A is for auk
who lives by the sea,

Bb

B is for beaver
felling a tree.

Cc

C is for caterpillar
who eats a lot,

Dd

D is for dragonfly
flitting by when it's hot.

Ee

E is for eagle
seeking salmon to eat,

Ff

F is for frog
with webbed hind feet.

Gg

G is for goose
paddling under a bridge,

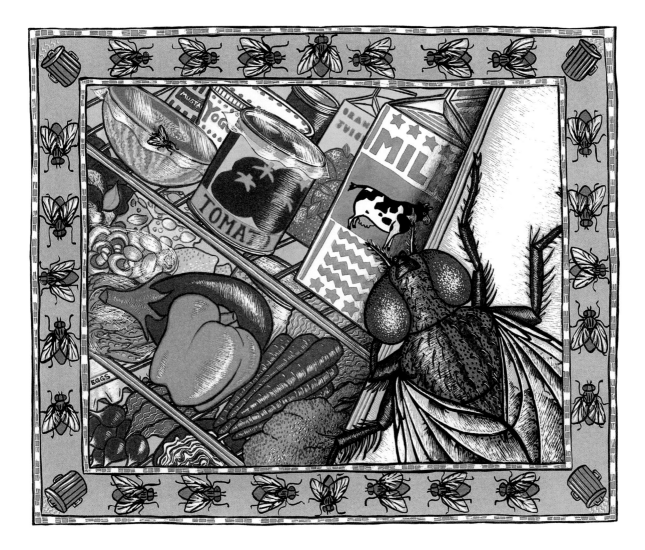

Hh

H is for housefly
inspecting your fridge.

Ii

I is for inchworm
sneaking along the ground,

Jj

J is for jumping mouse
hopping around.

Kk

K is for killer whale
in the deep blue sea,

Ll

L is for loon
who swims excellently.

Mm

M is for moose
munching plants in a park,

Nn

N is for nighthawk
catching bugs in the dark.

Oo

O is for otter—
look at him go!

Pp

P is for polar bear
walking on snow.

Qq

Q is for queen bee
laying eggs to hatch,

Rr

R is for raccoon—
see her lifting the latch?

Ss

S is for salmon
swimming up a creek,

Tt

T is for turtle—
her mouth is a beak.

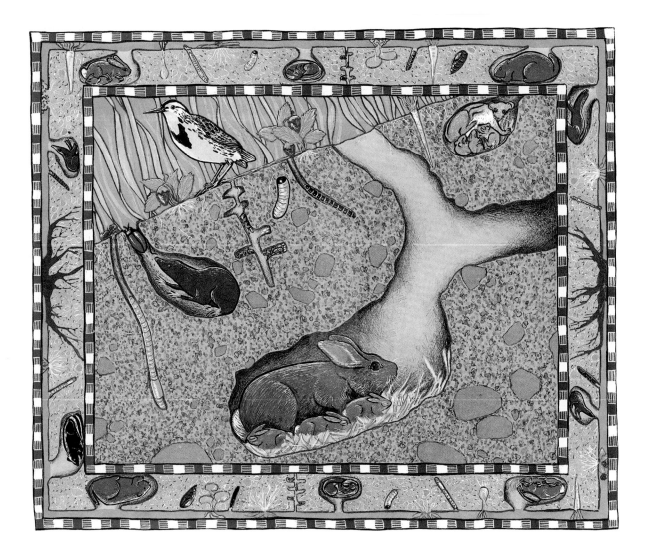

Uu

U is for underground.
Who lives there?

Vv

V is for vole
who had better beware!

Ww

W is for whooping crane
wading near shore,

Xx

X is for x-ray
of a big dinosaur.

Yy

Y is for yellowjacket
who might live near you,

Zz

And Z is for zoo!
Can you tell who's who?

Nature Notes

Aa Great Auk
with a colony of gannets

Although there are several smaller species of auk still found in the North Atlantic, the great auk is now extinct because of over-hunting. These large, flightless birds were easy prey out of the water and their eggs were collected for food. The last known pair was killed in 1844. Beside them was found a single broken egg.

Bb Beaver
with a woolly caterpillar, swimming beaver, great blue heron

The beaver, which is the second largest rodent in the world, has chisel-like, self-sharpening teeth that it uses to cut down trees, remove branches, and strip off bark. After they eat the bark, beavers build dams and lodges with the stripped trees. A beaver's flat tail acts like a rudder in water, helps the beaver balance upright while felling trees, and is slapped loudly on the water's surface to warn the family when danger threatens.

Cc Black Swallowtail Caterpillar
with eggs, chrysalis, adult butterfly

Caterpillars hatch from eggs laid by butterflies and moths. In this, the second of its four life stages, the insect devours large quantities of plant matter. Because the black swallowtail caterpillar prefers plants such as cultivated carrots, parsley, celery, and dill, it is often found in backyard gardens. Over several weeks of intense feeding, the caterpillar increases greatly in size before pupating into a chrysalis. There the adult develops, emerging finally as a butterfly.

Dd Dragonfly
with mergansers and pickerelweed

Dragonflies, with their large eyes, movable heads, and ability to fly both forward and backward, catch huge numbers of mosquitoes and other flying insects. Their eggs, usually deposited on the water, hatch into naiads, the dragonfly's larvae. After several years of eating other aquatic creatures, the naiad crawls out of the water and the fully formed adult emerges from a slit in its back.

Ee Bald Eagle
with eaglets in nest, humpback whales breaching, sea lions basking

Bald eagles, who mate for life, build huge nests (some weigh two tons) in tall trees. The young eaglets are fed fish, which their parents catch with their long, curved claws. After the eaglets grow their first dark brown feathers, they learn to fly by exercising on the wide platform of their nest. The bald eagle has been an endangered species in many areas because much of the forest in which they find nesting trees has been cut down for lumber or development.

Ff Leopard Frog
with a ladybug, ant, white admiral butterfly

The leopard frog begins life underwater as one of a mass of jelly-protected eggs. It hatches into a tiny tadpole, which breathes through gills like a fish. Eventually, legs and lungs develop and soon after the tail is reabsorbed into the body to feed the final metamorphosis of tadpole into frog, who can leave the water to breathe on land. The leopard frog has long, muscular hind legs for hopping, and webbed feet for swimming, so that it can escape predators both on land and in the water.

Gg Canada Goose
with a black squirrel and cardinal

The unmistakable honks of Canada geese ringing across the sky as they migrate in V-formation inspired the Cree Indians to call them "hounds of heaven." In the spring, while the goose sits on her two to nine eggs, her mate for life (the gander) stays close by on guard. When the hatchlings appear, both parents stand near so the goslings will recognize them in the future and, because the young identify with the first creature they see, will realize that they too are geese. In the following weeks, the downy yellow brood, which can leave the nest right away, will learn by imitating their parents.

Hh Housefly
in its common habitat

Because they can easily adapt to different environments, houseflies are found all over the world. Their large, curved, compound eyes are made up of about 4,000 hexagonal lenses, each of which points in a slightly different direction so that each sees only part of an object. This confusion of images is joined together in the fly's brain, making one coherent picture. The housefly's two single wings, which distinguish it from other flying insects, can beat 200 times a second.

Ii Inchworm
with a monarch butterfly, nuthatch, asters, milkweed, burdock, plantain, goldenrod, dock

Inchworms, also known as measuring worms or loopers, are the larvae of one of the largest families of moths. Their unique way of moving developed because of their lack of legs in the middle segments of their bodies. Some inchworms resemble twigs when they grip a branch with their hind legs and let their long bodies project out on an angle. If they keep perfectly still, this trick of mimicry can fool predators.

Jj Woodland Jumping Mouse
with a moth and owl

The woodland jumping mouse has large hind legs and a tail longer than its body to help it balance when leaping about—sometimes 2 m (6 ft.) in a single bound. Good swimmers, woodland jumping mice live in burrows close to water, eating seeds, berries, and insects. They are most active at night, when they must be wary of owls, one of their major predators.

Kk Killer Whale
with herring gulls

The highly intelligent killer whales, some 8 m (25 ft.) long and weighing six tons, travel in pods of three to 50 animals—although about 10 is the most common number. These tight-knit family groups can be told apart by the different noises, calls, and piercing sounds they make. They eat mostly cod, herring, and salmon, but will also hunt sea birds or seals, and on occasion will even attack other whales.

Ll Loon
with lake trout and yellow perch

On clear northern lakes in the summer, the cackling, yodeling, and haunting wails of the loon are a familiar sound. Such specialized diving birds that they cannot walk properly on land, loons are very fast and agile underwater, capable of traveling several hundred meters (feet) before surfacing for air. Their diet consists mainly of fish, but they also eat leeches, crayfish, and frogs. Although loon chicks can dive within a day of hatching, they are fed by their parents for several months. If danger threatens, the chicks are carried away on a parent's back or tucked under a wing.

Mm Moose
with a diving kingfisher, flicker on tree trunk, dragonfly

In the summer, moose are often seen feeding on underwater and floating plants such as pond lilies. Excellent swimmers and divers, it is not unusual for them to stay submerged for a full minute or to swim across a wide lake. The distinctive antlers of the males, which can span 2 m (6 ft.), grow anew each year. After shedding the velvety skin that feeds their growth, the antlers fall off in the fall and a new set begins growing in by spring.

Nn Nighthawk
with bats, luna moth

Nighthawks, which are not true hawks, are most often seen at twilight and after dark, flitting high above city buildings or over open fields. Flying with their huge mouths agape, they can capture large numbers of mosquitoes in a single snap or snatch up a large moth. Nighthawks have adapted easily to city life, laying their eggs on gravel-covered roofs, perfect camouflage for the mottled coloring of the shells.

Oo River Otter
with rose-breasted grosbeaks, white-tailed deer, two otters in the river

River otters, long and streamlined with webbed feet and waterproof fur, are wonderful swimmers, spending much of their time in water frolicking and catching fish. They are playful all their lives, and enjoy slipping down mudslides in the summer and sliding down snow banks in the winter. Two cubs are born each spring in a riverbank tunnel. The cubs stay with their mother a long time, learning from her the skills they will need to survive on their own.

Pp Polar Bear
with cubs, Arctic hare, snowy owl

In the fall, the female polar bear digs a snug den in a snowdrift. There she gives birth to two cubs weighing barely 0.5 kg (1 lb.) each. In the early spring, when the cubs have grown to about 12 kg (25 lb.), the mother brings them outside. They will stay with her for two years, traveling great distances across the Arctic landscape, learning to hunt seals for themselves.

Qq Queen Honeybees
with attendant workers

Although there may be several thousand worker bees and several hundred male drones in a hive, there is only one queen. Attended by workers, the queen can lay 1,000 eggs a day. When the eggs hatch, some of the larvae are chosen to become queens and are fed a special diet of "royal jelly" instead of the worker mixture of pollen and honey. In the late spring, the reigning queen leaves the hive with a swarm of workers to found a new colony. Soon after her departure, the first young queen to emerge takes the old queen's place.

Rr Raccoon
with young

The raccoon roams at night and is an omnivore, meaning it will eat almost anything. In the wild its favorite foods are crayfish, bird and turtle eggs, freshwater clams, nuts, and seeds. The young, born in the spring, spend as long as a year with their mother. The raccoon has adapted easily to urban life, showing dexterity and ingenuity in opening doors, latches, and garbage can lids to get at food inside.

Ss Sockeye Salmon
two males, one female

Salmon lay and fertilize their eggs in the same freshwater spawning grounds where they themselves originated. After the eggs hatch, the young salmon spend one to three years in freshwater before swimming to the sea, where they remain for several more years. When the time comes for them to make their return journey to the breeding streams, sockeye salmon change color from silvery blue-green to red, and their heads turn green. The male grows a hump on its back and its jaws enlarge. Both male and females swim vast distances—battling currents, jumping up waterfalls, and evading natural enemies such as grizzly bears—to reach the spawning grounds where the cycle begins anew.

Tt Snapping Turtle
with minnows and brook trout

The snapping turtle, which lives in ponds, marshes, rivers, and lakes, has a long, flexible neck and sharp, powerful jaws that help it catch food. It eats fish, frogs, small mammals, waterfowl, and plants, and is also a good scavenger. Although the snapping turtle can be aggressive on land where it is vulnerable to attack, in its water habitat it is usually shy and unthreatening to humans.

Uu Underground
with a meadowlark, earthworm, shrew chasing beetle, ants, larva, millipede, cottontail rabbits, field mice

Many creatures spend at least part of their lives underground. Earthworms tunnel constantly, passing large quantities of earth through their bodies, digesting only the dead plant material they need. The shrew digs for insects, its favorite food. Ant colonies build networks of tunnels joined to storerooms and nurseries. Other insects spend either their larval stage (some eating tender root tips) or pupal stage underground. Some mammals, such as mice, dig burrows where they store food, nest, and sleep, protected from above-ground enemies. The cottontail, instead of digging for itself, takes over another animal's abandoned burrow to nest in.

Vv Meadow Vole
with a fox, hare, red-tailed hawk

Meadow voles live in fields, eating seeds and vegetation. They are fast breeders, producing large litters, which mature quickly. Unchecked, a single pair of voles can have 200 descendants in a year. Some years are called "vole years" when the vole population skyrockets, attracting many predators such as hawks, owls, and foxes. To make their movement from place to place almost invisible from above, voles make covered runways—in the summer they trample grass and eat away only the lower stems of plants along their routes, and in the winter they dig tunnels through the snow.

Ww Whooping Crane
with a monarch butterfly, dragonfly, turtle

Whooping cranes have a remarkable courtship dance, which few people have opportunity to witness because this bird is so rare. In the early 20th century, hunting and the destruction of its habitat decimated the species, and by the 1960s there were fewer than 20 left worldwide. Fortunately, with help, their numbers are currently climbing, and more whoopers complete the southerly migration to their wintering grounds each year. This majestic bird has a very long, coiled trachea, which enables it to make a loud trumpet call that carries across vast distances.

Xx X-ray of Triceratops
with a Stegosaurus, Tyrannosaurus, Hadrosaurs hatching, Sauropods grazing

During the Mesozoic era, 225 to 65 million years ago, dinosaurs were the dominant animals on Earth. These reptiles came in all different sizes, some tiny, others 30 m (100 ft.) long. Many dinosaurs, such as the Stegosaurs, Triceratops, Sauropods, and Hadrosaurs, were plant-eaters, while others, such as the Tyrannosaurs, were meat-eaters. The dinosaurs died out 65 million years ago. Many scientists believe this was due to a climate change the dinosaurs could not adjust to.

Yy Yellowjacket Wasp
with a garden spider and barn swallows

Colonies of yellowjackets, a common type of wasp, are primarily made up of egg-laying queens and female workers. Late in the season a few males arrive to fertilize young queens who, unlike the others, hibernate over winter. In the spring, the young queens build "starter" nests with "wasp paper" (chewed-up wood bits mixed with saliva), which their offspring will complete over the summer. By early fall, the nest may contain several thousand cells and 2,000 wasps, all of whom will die except the few select young queens.

Zz Zoo
full of the animals you met in these pages

A zoo is a place of discovery, where animals are exhibited for people to view them. It is also a place where scientists can study animals up close, and conservationists who work to protect animals can learn what the animals need in order to survive in the wild. Zoos can't hope to save all endangered species, but they do what they can to protect wild animals from around the world and their wild homes.

Zz
Zoo (border repeats animals A to Z)

1. Ruby-Throated Hummingbird
2. Brown Bat
3. Zebra Butterfly
4. American Redstart
5. Chickadee
6. Grizzly Bear
7. Magpie
8. Walrus
9. Groundhog
10. White-Tailed Deer
11. Mountain Goat
12. Pronghorn Antelope
13. Caribou
14. Muskox
15. Pileated Woodpecker
16. Wolf
17. Bighorn Sheep
18. Bobcat
19. Porcupine
20. Skunk
21. Barn Owl
22. Opossum with young
23. Hare
24. Badger
25. Massasauga Rattler
26. Toad
27. Box Turtle
28. Wood Duck
29. Yellow Perch
30. Brook Trout
31. Painted Turtle
32. Lake Sturgeon
33. Crayfish